# PITTOWN

A SPIRITUAL FICTION SERIES

WALDMEER SERIES
BOOK 5

DONNA GODDARD

Second Edition 2023

Published by Donna Goddard

Victoria, Australia

Paperback ISBN: 978-0645729641

Large Print ISBN: 978-1764151139

Cover design by Donna Goddard

www.donnagoddard.com

# CONTENTS

# DIRTY DANCING

## REPEAT OR DELETE

PART II
# SILENT ORDER

## JOE-JOE'S APARTMENTS

## STORE CREEK

## LOVERS, FAIRIES, AND FOOLS

## HIDDEN ENTRANCE

## RETURN OF THE WARRIORS

# PART I

# IMPERMANENCE

# REMARKABLY ORDINARY

# CHAPTER 1
# ORDINARY

*Twenty years later:*

Before her eyes opened, Merlyn sensed the soft, red glow behind the makeshift curtain, which hung unevenly over the window. The unit was relatively modern and clean, and had heating and cooling that worked. Pittown, as a suburb, was ordinary, but she could afford the rent on her own.

*Remarkably ordinary*, thought Merlyn as she walked a couple of doors to the one decent cafe.

The owner had only warmed to her once in the few weeks that she had been going there. He was a big, dark, bearded guy with a good business head and a soft heart behind the all-man demeanour. Merlyn knew this by how he related to the children who came into the cafe. He was a family man.

"Good to see you," said the owner enthusiastically on that one rare occasion, as if that was how he always spoke to Merlyn. She had been sitting with a male friend who came to see her new place. The owner then talked to them both as if they were his longtime friends. Merlyn surmised that, in his mind, women should not be made friends of unless they were attached to a male. She wondered if he thought the friend was her husband.

This morning, he didn't look up from the coffee machine.

The cafe made a valiant effort to keep up with the fashionable cafes a mere suburb or two away. Thanks to the young manager, their social media was on point, with photos of smiling people, spoiled dogs, food, and light.

Nevertheless, the working-class origins of the place were never far away. For one thing, they opened at 6 a.m. to accommodate the tradies. As Merlyn was an early riser, she often took advantage of the early opening time.

At that hour, the place was full of men. They would glance at her, modify their language (usually), and return to their conversations. She looked at the fluorescent-vested, heavy-booted men standing in the takeaway line.

*Goodness only knows what they are talking about,* she thought. *What do tradies talk about all day?*

She didn't know. She smiled at the memory of those happening cafes closer to the city.

*When those cafes are full of men, half of them are gay,* she mused.

She considered them more interesting than the hurley-burleys before her.

*But this is where I am,* she told herself as she walked out of the cafe and down to the lake at the bottom of her street. *This is where I am, so I give myself to here.*

## CHAPTER 2
## LAKESIDE VIEW

Merlyn's street was called Lakeside View. It was a somewhat pretentious name. There was indeed a lake, which was quite large for a city suburb. Several sports ovals and revegetation areas surrounded it, making it open enough for broad sweeps of sky to be seen. The view was admittedly flanked by a row of massive electric towers.

*The sky is important*, thought Merlyn, *even if it has to be viewed through steel latticework.*

Messy houses followed the path of the power lines. Merlyn felt that the inhabitants of those houses had other things on their minds than the EMFs from power lines. They did not notice the towers, but nor did they notice the sky, the lake, or any of the feathered neighbours that called the lake home.

Noticed or not, Mother Nature was given a little space to breathe, and breathe she did. The ducks, cormorants, and swamp-hens manoeuvred through the plastic and oil that floated amongst the weeds.

*She is fighting,* thought Merlyn. *Giving it her all. Gotta respect that.*

# THE SLEEPING PROPHET

## CHAPTER 3
## BENJAMIN

Although the Pittown cafe owner had misjudged Merlyn's friend to be her husband, she did have a husband—an estranged husband, anyway. The estrangement was how she came to be living in Pittown.

Merlyn and Benjamin had only been married for three years. It wasn't long, but as it turned out, long enough.

They had known each other for two years before getting married. Merlyn wasn't a big fan of getting married, but Benjamin had fallen in love with her and wanted the marriage to work.

For her part, Merlyn both loved and was in love with Benjamin. However, she knew he was ill-prepared for the reality of a committed relationship. She also knew that love is the most powerful force in the universe, so she gave Benjamin and the marriage her best shot and put her faith in his love to get him through.

"Do you even like me?" said Benjamin accusingly on their last night together.

Merlyn looked at him and felt she often didn't like the person he could be to her.

Not wanting to shy away from an honest answer, she said, "Who would...?"

She was going to say, *Who would like being treated the way you treat me?*

However, Benjamin interrupted.

"Right," said Benjamin. "That's fantastic. You don't even like me. Then there is no point being together."

If it had been earlier in the marriage, Merlyn would have tried to help him understand what she was saying. He wasn't easy to talk to. Oh, he could talk, alright. He was a rather dreadful gossip, although he considered himself the opposite. He could tell a very amusing story. If he had no vested interest, he could kindly listen to other people's problems and even give them good advice (which they often took). He could talk endlessly about nothing with people who also liked to talk about nothing (something Merlyn couldn't tolerate, finding it beyond boring).

However, when it came to talking about the important personal things in life, Benjamin was neither equipped nor willing to learn how to do it. If Merlyn tried to coax him into talking about some prickly issue, he was fond of saying, "You know that we have discussed this numerous times before, in great detail, and I don't wish to discuss it again!" Mind you, the "numerous times" would have been one time. And the "in great detail" would have been him pontificating about Merlyn's less-than-desirable behaviour.

Like many, if not most, people, he had never learned to

talk properly. He thought it was a dangerous endeavour that would likely take you somewhere regrettable.

When he drank, which he frequently did, he was more talkative. Although *a drunk man's words are a sober man's thoughts,* as the saying goes, both the words and thoughts were muddled and destructive, as is generally the case with drinkers and talkers.

"Tomorrow, I'll look for a place in Pittown near my new job," said Merlyn with resignation. "I'll be able to afford it there on my own. You should be able to stay here on your own."

She paused and added, "Or you can get someone else to share the rent with you."

With more than a bit of spite, Benjamin said, "Yes, I'll get someone else. I can think of heaps of people who'd like to share with me."

Indeed, there were.

## CHAPTER 4
## EDGAR AND ENID

A few months before moving to Pittown, Merlyn started a job caring for an elderly woman named Enid, who had a stroke that left her with intermittent memory loss. Her highly successful son, Edgar, wanted his mother to live in her own home as she was happier there. He slept there but needed someone to be with her during the day. Edgar's advertisement for the position was short and specific.

**Daytime carer needed for elderly lady.**
**Must be kind. Must have impeccable integrity.**

The wording of the advertisement was why Merlyn applied for the job. She thought that anyone asking for kindness and integrity must be that themselves.

The interview was a little odd. Edgar opened the door and looked at her searchingly as if he was running through a computer program in his mind, a checklist only known to him. On entering the old-fashioned but sweet and clean lounge room, Merlyn gave Edgar her resume. He put it on the table without looking at it. Then, after a few half-hearted questions, he stood up to indicate the interview was over.

"My mother is special," said Edgar as he politely opened the front door. "She needs..."

"...special care," volunteered Merlyn.

Edgar nodded. Merlyn could see the sadness in his eyes that this special woman was only intermittently there now.

"You will let me know after interviewing all the applicants?" asked Merlyn.

"No," said Edgar. "I didn't accept anyone else's application. You will start tomorrow if that is convenient."

Convenient or not, Edgar was not the type of person you inconvenienced.

## CHAPTER 5
## PROPHET HOUSE

"I named Edgar after Edgar Cayce," said Enid to Merlyn during one of her lucid conversations. "Do you know who that is?"

"No," said Merlyn.

"He was a wonderful clairvoyant," said Enid. "He would go into a trance and give long speeches about life and everything important. His secretary took it all down for decades. They called him the Sleeping Prophet because of how he got his information."

"Really?" said Merlyn, who was genuinely fascinated.

"Edgar and I sometimes laugh that my Edgar is the Waking Profit, not the Sleeping Prophet," said Enid.

Her laugh was pure and infectious. She seemed to laugh along with life.

Seeing Merlyn's confused look, Enid said, "Because of his business, dear, his finance company—Prophet House."

She added proudly, "It's one of the country's leading businesses now."

Edgar was an unusual mix of person—gentle and intuitive with a sharp, demanding intelligence. He was intensely interested in the world of making money. The strange thing was that Edgar didn't seem that interested in money. He did have an expensive apartment in a prestigious bayside suburb, but he appeared as content, if not more, in his mother's house in Pittown.

Sensing Merlyn's thoughts, Enid said, "We all have different things to do in life. It drives us and won't let us go."

Enid laughed and said, "The damn thing just won't leave us alone."

Her lucidity then drifted into the ether, and she started rambling incoherent memories of Edgar as a boy. She asked Merlyn if Edgar was outside playing. Merlyn replied that she would go and look. She went to the kitchen and made a pot of tea, Earl Grey with milk, the way Enid liked.

"Here, love," said Merlyn. "While Edgar plays, let's have a nice cup of tea and look out the window at your flowers."

Enid's house was one of the well-cared-for ones in Pittown. It was within walking distance of Merlyn's unit. In years gone by, every spring, Enid planted hundreds of pansies in her front garden. It was somewhat unimaginative, but there was so much love in the garden that she could pull it off. These days, Edgar organised a gardener to plant the pansies. Enid thought she did it herself.

"I love my flowers," said Enid wistfully. "I like Edgar to have something beautiful to look at while he is growing up. Beauty is the soul of life. If we learn to see beauty, we are never far from God."

Even in her confused moments, Enid didn't seem to lose her connection with her higher self. Only her lower self got confused.

She looked at Merlyn and said, "Who are you again? You have a lovely face."

Merlyn smiled and said, "I'm your friend."

Enid relaxed and closed her eyes for a rest.

*Perhaps,* thought Merlyn, *she's visiting the Sleeping Prophet.*

# THE MOVING BUDDHA

## CHAPTER 6
## UNEXPECTED

"It's good for the money," said Benjamin, glancing around Merlyn's Pittown unit.

He wanted her to have a decent place because he was decent. Relationships are a different thing. *Decent* can go out the window. Sometimes, it should. Yesterday, Merlyn messaged Ben and asked him to visit.

"How's your new job?" asked Benjamin.

"The lady is adorable," said Merlyn.

"And the son?" asked Benjamin.

"Just as lovely but more reserved," said Merlyn. "I don't see him much. Only at handover."

Benjamin nodded. The undercurrent was starting to swirl. Merlyn felt it best to get to the point.

"I'm pregnant."

The colour drained from Ben's face. Then, he frowned.

Before he had a chance to say anything, Merlyn continued, "Remember our second last night together?"

It was probably goodbye sex, although neither knew it at the time. In their last year together, they had only had sex a few times. That wasn't Merlyn's doing. It was Ben's. When things weren't smooth sailing, Ben's go-to was to be withholding. Withholding of his body and anything else he thought might be of value.

After separating, Merlyn assumed that the lack of a period was her body adjusting post-pill. She felt a little unwell but thought it was the stress of separating, moving, and finding a new job. There were a couple of times when she had forgotten to take the pill in their last months together, but as they didn't have an active sex life by that stage, she didn't give it a second thought. A second thought, in retrospect, may have been wise.

As Ben didn't say anything, Merlyn asked, "How do you feel about it?"

Ben straightened his spine and said with a mixture of courage and blame, "How I feel doesn't matter at this point."

Merlyn wasn't sure what he meant.

Seeing her look, he added, "Because you don't get a choice once a child is involved."

Merlyn nodded. "Whatever problems we have had," she said, "I don't want to think about them anymore. There are other things to think about now."

Over the following week, Ben wasn't nearly as worried or upset about it as he had assumed he would be. Acceptance is easier when one is powerless. Besides, it meant that, come what may, Merlyn would still be somewhere in his life.

# CHAPTER 7
# IMPERMANENCE

Pittown Hospital's new and enthusiastic volunteer committee was doing its best to update and beautify the hospital. Unfortunately, as is often the case on such committees, there was a raging battle between two of the committee's strongest personalities.

The argument had come to a head over the Buddha statue in the Zen garden. The garden was the committee's pièce de résistance. Trendy and innovative, the small area was a place of serenity with its well-placed rocks, carefully sculptured sand, rows of azaleas, and a glorious Japanese maple.

"The statue is the garden's highlight," insisted one of the combating committee parties. "The people love him. He encapsulates the whole feeling of the garden, which is, may I remind you, meditation and introspection in this challenging environment of the hospital."

She considered herself an expert on Zen Buddhism and Zen gardens. So did her opponent.

"I beg to differ," he said with feigned tolerance.

"Respected scholars of philosophy know that Zen gardens and Buddha statues do not belong together. The garden draws the eye outwards towards the Infinite. The statue draws the eye inwards towards reflection. They work against each other. While they are both of value, they conflict with each other."

As neither would concede and outright war seemed tactless, they had resorted to commanding the groundsmen to move the statue into the storage shed or back into the middle of the garden according to their point of view. As a result, the hospital staff affectionately referred to the statue as the Moving Buddha.

This evening, Ben was in the hospital lift and looked at the Buddha statue on the trolley. It looked serene despite its unceremonious transportation.

The groundsman laughed and said, "He's pretty damn calm about being pushed all over the place. Nothin' fazes him."

Ben laughed, although he didn't feel like it much. Merlyn miscarried last night. Standing at the door of her hospital room, he wondered what state she would be in. Would it have been painful? Was it still so? On entering, he was relieved that she looked pale but otherwise okay.

"The doctor said it was a little boy," she said softly. "I'm so sorry."

"Don't be silly," said Ben. "What are you sorry for?"

"I feel that I have failed the baby," said Merlyn. "I'm his mother. I should have been able to do something. That's what mothers do. They fix things up."

Everything Ben thought of saying seemed trite. On the way back to the hospital foyer, he decided to follow the signs leading to the rooftop Zen garden. He wondered who drew the precise spiral and ripple patterns in the sand. They looked so impermanent. No sooner would they be raked, and the wind and rain would surely come and disturb the whole thing.

*I guess you couldn't be too attached to whatever you made in the sand,* he thought.

Sitting on one of the wooden benches, he gazed towards the large boulders. Some were lying down. A few were upright. He felt they must have been placed strategically, but he couldn't see the pattern. His eyes followed a line of azaleas and rested on the glowing, red Maple tree in the centre of the garden. Buddha was sitting undisturbed beneath it.

"I see you got your spot back," said Ben.

It didn't feel strange to talk to the statue because it seemed to be there for that. Ben thought about the many people in the hospital below him and again spoke to the statue.

"I suppose a hospital has as much death as it does birth, as much illness as it does recovery, and as much suffering as it does healing."

As he was leaving, Ben noticed that behind the garden wall was a plaque that read,

*Here, in the garden,*
*in this quiet space,*
*lie little lives*
*not long for this place.*

*Go home, sweet ones,*
*you're saved a lot of strife.*
*We, who remain,*
*will not forget your life.*

It was a burial ground for miscarried foetuses.
*Tomorrow,* thought Ben, *I will tell Merlyn.*

# EDGARS LAKE

## CHAPTER 8
## EDGAR I AND II

E dgar was not only named after the famous clairvoyant Edgar Cayce, but also after his great-grandfather, Edgar I, who lived in Pittown his entire life.

~

IN THOSE DAYS, Pittown was an agricultural area. Edgar I built a concrete weir and dammed the creek running through his rural Pittown property, creating a lake for wildlife. He bequeathed that part of his property to the people of Pittown, and it was aptly named Edgars Lake (the lake at the bottom of Merlyn's street).

Over time, Pittown became a more populated residential and industrial area. At that stage, the industries were unrestrained by anti-pollution laws. The lake became contaminated, the fish died, and the birdlife went elsewhere.

Eventually, Edgar I's granddaughter, Enid, formed a committee to clean up the lake. They lobbied the government for funds to continue their work. The lake was drained, and the weir was repaired, which improved the water flow. A low-flow bypass wetlands area was created to assist with silt buildup. Litter traps were installed, and eventually, the wildlife returned. Although the lake still had some rubbish, it was a far cry from its ruined state before Enid's work.

*BACK TO CURRENT PITTOWN:*

Merlyn had taken to making Edgar II's dinner (along with Enid's) and leaving it in the fridge. He wasn't much of a cook and usually ordered takeaway when he arrived home from work. She told him it was no trouble. She knew how tiring it would be to work all day and then be tied to his mother's needs as soon as he came home. It wasn't maintainable, but Edgar said he would do it for now. He appreciated Merlyn's kindness.

## CHAPTER 9
## FIRM FRIENDS

One evening, seeing how tired Edgar was on returning to his mother's house, Merlyn said, "Why don't you go for a walk down to your great-grandfather's lake?"

"I can't hold you up any longer," said Edgar, who was already late home.

Merlyn saw the foggy look in Edgar's eyes and said, "Please, I'm fine. I have no one at home. The fresh air will blow away the cobwebs."

Feeling too tired to object, Edgar set off for a walk and returned a new man. From that day, Merlyn and Edgar became firm friends.

Regardless of their different positions in life, they were equal in friendship. Both were intelligent (in different ways). They enjoyed talking to one another. The area of intelligence that they had in common was their ability to read people. They were similarly insightful, astute, and telepathic.

Edgar began running business ideas past Merlyn. He

didn't ask her about the technicalities of the financial world, of which she knew nothing. Instead, he asked her how she thought ordinary people would react to things he wanted to do in his business. He was conscious of providing an excellent service to the average, financially illiterate person. Edgar not only asked Merlyn's opinion, but he listened carefully to her response. He asked things like:

*What do you think people think this word means?*

*What do you think of this idea?*

He showed her videos of CEOs of companies he was considering investing in and asked for her thoughts about the person:

*Do you think he's smart?*

*Do you think she's ethical?*

*Do you think he's passionate about the business?*

*Do you think he's mentally stable?*

Edgar wasn't possessive and asked Merlyn about her relationships quite openly. Generally, people ask such questions to assess whether someone else is a threat. When around Edgar, Merlyn tended to think of all the good and funny things Ben did, so that is how she spoke of him. She didn't tell Edgar about her recent miscarriage.

Merlyn and Edgar's relationship was exceptionally harmonious. Both were naturally geared towards peaceful relationships, and neither gave the other any reason for an argument.

Further, neither found the other draining in the slightest. They enjoyed each other's company without feeling something had been taken from them. It was probably the easiest, most harmonious relationship they would ever experience.

One would assume they would have considered a couple relationship as they were both single and similarly aged.

Neither did. As intuitive as they were about other people, they were likewise about themselves.

Perhaps it was that they were too similar. Perhaps they didn't need each other. Perhaps there were other people for them. Whatever the reason, it did not seriously enter their minds to be more than friends. Thus, their friendship retained its purity of intention unhampered by the complex motives of couple relationships.

# MOVING ON

## CHAPTER 10
## DIFFERENT AND BETTER

Although there were nicer shops a suburb or two closer to the city, Merlyn made a point of shopping at the Pittown ones. It seemed to her disloyal not to use them. Besides, she found the people interesting.

Not infrequently, someone walked past her and turned their head to give her a second look. They looked like they thought they knew her, but then decided they didn't. Sometimes, they looked at her quizzically as if they thought she didn't belong in Pittown.

Merlyn had grown up in a similar suburb to Pittown, although much water had flowed under the bridge since then. She knew what life felt like in a place like this.

What most struck her about the average Pittown resident was the dulled look of acceptance that sat in their eyes. It wasn't the acceptance of a peaceful mind. It was the acceptance that shouldn't be accepting, when fire is needed instead—fire to educate oneself, to create a better life, to move and not come back, to do something!

*Before anyone can improve their life,* thought Merlyn as she walked along the main shopping strip, *they must get the idea that change is possible, that life can be different and better, and that it is worth the effort it takes to make it happen.*

She picked up some rubbish that had blown in front of her and put it in the bin. Since moving to Pittown, Merlyn had been forever picking up rubbish.

## CHAPTER 11
## CROSSING-OVER

E nid was becoming less lucid. Edgar was becoming more exhausted.

"I think the time is soon," said Merlyn when Edgar asked how his mother had been that day.

Edgar looked anxious.

"Time for your mother to go into a home," clarified Merlyn. "She's not getting much from being here in her home. She sleeps a lot and doesn't want to go outside into the garden. She doesn't even want to look out the window. You can't keep looking after her at night and working all day. Something is going to give."

Merlyn wondered if Enid had deliberately decided to decline. A few weeks ago, she told Merlyn that Edgar was looking terribly tired and that she didn't want to be a burden to him. Merlyn didn't tell Edgar about his mother's comment, but from that day, Enid wasn't the same. She wasn't interested in eating. She didn't have the conscious moments she had been having previously. Her eyes seemed far away. Merlyn felt that she was beginning the process of crossing over.

"I'm not sure how much she is with us anymore," said Merlyn gently.

The next evening, Edgar told Merlyn that he had been speaking to nursing homes during the day and that one lovely (and expensive) one had been arranged close to his bayside apartment.

## CHAPTER 12
## FATHER FRANCIS

"I'm afraid it is only a temporary job," said Father Francis. "I'm leaving in a few months, and, as yet, there is no replacement for me at Saint Xavier's."

Merlyn watched him carefully. Father Francis was about fifty. He was immediately likeable and had the calm composure of someone who had been in the public eye for a long time. Father Francis's Italian heritage would have matched the cultural background of most of his Pittown parishioners. The temporary housekeeping job in the Catholic presbytery suited Merlyn after Enid transitioned to the nursing home.

At the end of Merlyn's second week at the presbytery, a woman she had seen visiting numerous times was crying quietly in the hallway.

"I'm sorry," said Merlyn, "Father Francis is out at the moment."

The woman looked inconsolable. Merlyn wasn't sure that even Father Francis could help with that sort of distress.

"No, no," said the woman, "it's I who is sorry. I shouldn't be crying, especially here."

She pointed around the presbytery to indicate sacred ground.

Extending her hand with the warmth of a long-time mother and wife, she said, "I'm Martha."

The presbytery was very quiet. It had the feeling of a building preparing for inevitable evacuation—functional but lacking life and brightness.

"It's sad to think that no one will live in this old building," said Martha.

Merlyn nodded, but as she didn't have any attachment to the building or Father Francis, she didn't feel sad at all. Martha, however, seemed to have a profound attachment to both. She sat in a nearby chair and began a story that both knew, once started, needed to be finished.

"Today is my last day here," said Martha. "My daughter is picking me up tonight, and I am moving north to her house indefinitely. I never speak about Francis because... well, you know."

Merlyn didn't know. She wasn't an insider to the intricacies and implications of Catholic Church politics.

"My husband died when I was thirty-five," said Martha. "We had many marital problems, but it wasn't too bad as far as marriages go. We were friends, still lovers. That counts for a lot."

Martha had a grounded, straightforward approach to life and people that would have endeared her to those who needed it. Merlyn sensed that Father Francis was one of those in need.

"I was left with three primary-aged children," said Martha. "My husband and I already knew Francis as we were highly involved in the local Catholic church."

"Francis is an extraordinary man," said Martha as she looked at Merlyn with grey pools of eyes.

Merlyn wasn't so sure that Francis was as extraordinary as Martha thought, but there was no doubt that, in Martha's mind, he was a truly unique person.

"Francis was also thirty-five when my husband died. He had already been a priest for a long time."

A hint of smile passed over Martha's lips, and she repeated, "A long time."

Suddenly, Merlyn saw it. Martha was Father Francis's lover. She would have had all the experience, warmth, and life energy of a woman of the world. Father Francis would have had all the desire, devotion, and innocence of a man who needed a woman. Not any woman, but a kind, spiritual one who knew what she was doing and could also keep her mouth shut.

"For fifteen years, I have been silent. So important," said Martha, looking at the pictures of past parish priests lining the wall. "Even if it killed me, I would be silent."

Given the look on her face, Merlyn thought it probably was killing her.

"We loved each other," said Martha, "really loved each other. Sometimes, I couldn't quite keep up with him, if you know what I mean. We visited the most gorgeous places together. His days off were the best fun—gardens, museums, galleries, mountains, and the beach. In public, we were careful. It wasn't particularly hard because Francis is such an engaging person. He is one of those rare priests who has many friends, male and female."

Martha straightened her skirt and continued, "Once a week, on his night off, he stayed with me."

She stood up and paced to pacify the tears.

"He stayed with me for ten happy years," said Martha, "then things changed five years ago. He said he was so worried about the establishment finding out about our relationship that he should sleep in another room. I told him that it was fine. It wasn't fine, but I would have done anything to keep him with me."

*Oh, dear,* thought Merlyn. *Therein lies the problem.*

"I kept going," said Martha, with doom ringing from every syllable. "Not long ago, Francis told me he was going to leave the priesthood. I was thrilled and told myself that we could finally get married. Then he told me that he was going to marry someone else."

Martha looked blank, as if such news were impossible to process.

"My daughter has put her foot down and told me that enough is enough and that she is coming to get me."

Merlyn felt that words were powerless for such a profound hurt. She already knew Father Francis well enough to know that the last thing he would have wanted to do was to hurt someone, least of all his friend and lover of so long.

He probably persevered with the relationship, hoping to get Martha to detach from him and let him go. He would have seen it as the kindest thing to do. It wasn't kind. It gave Martha five years of wondering every day how she could get Francis back and make him love her again. Sometimes, she probably told herself that he did love her. But always, in her heart, she would have known it was over. That's not kind. It's torture.

*Father Francis mustn't want the church to know about his affair,* thought Merlyn.

He was leaving the priesthood with an excellent name, as

one of the golden ones, as a stable, emotionally available, genuinely devoted priest who had made the conscientious decision to leave the priesthood and begin a committed relationship with a woman. No one could complain about that. Except Martha, that is. And Martha's children.

*Dishonesty is a mistake,* thought Merlyn, *and Father Francis will have to carry that, but honesty wouldn't have stopped Martha's grief. Martha saw Francis as the best part of herself—irreplaceable and absolutely essential. That was her mistake, not his. We mustn't give that to anyone—saint or sinner, priest or common bloke on the street. Some things are not meant for giving away.*

# LOVE OF LIFE

## CHAPTER 13
## NAMES

Pittstop, the cafe near Merlyn, had been in the same family since it was a country stop for truckies. Sometimes, the owner's cousin, Tom, worked in the cafe. They were nothing alike.

"Can you remember my name?" asked Tom one day.

Merlyn usually didn't remember names well. However, she remembered people's energy exceptionally well.

"Yes," she said hesitantly.

"What is it?" asked Tom.

*He wants me to know who he is*, thought Merlyn. *He must want to be friends.*

Tom was the sort of person that many people would have wanted to befriend. Although he would have given the impression that he was friends with them all, he trusted few.

"It's Tom," said Merlyn.

Satisfied, Tom said, "I sometimes see you walking by the lake. I live on the other side of it."

Merlyn was surprised that Tom lived in Pittown. It didn't seem his sort of suburb.

"I normally work elsewhere, but I help my cousin out here sometimes," he said.

He was a good talker and also good at asking questions. He asked Merlyn many things other people wouldn't have bothered to ask. So, he found out things about her.

Recently, Tom told Merlyn that he lived with the love of his life.

"You live with someone?" said Merlyn.

"I'm terribly in love," said Tom dramatically. "I have never fallen so quickly and deeply in love."

Tom had a sweet side. He was also fond of using the f-word in his conversations. Merlyn didn't swear, and other people didn't tend to swear around her. Ben didn't swear at her even when he was angry. Tom wasn't swearing because he was angry. Nor was he swearing out of crassness (mind you, he was the first to thoroughly enjoy a crass conversation). Merlyn thought he did it deliberately, as if to say, *Come on. You're not so fragile that we can't swear to you. You're not a princess.*

"What's the name of the love of your life?" asked Merlyn.

"Hardy," said Tom. "He's from Brussels."

## CHAPTER 14
## SWANNING ABOUT

Merlyn watched the six little cygnets at Edgar's Lake with delight.

"I hope more of this lot survive," said a voice behind her.

It was a neighbour from the Friends of Edgars Lake. They had the zeal of missionaries.

"Last year, there were also six, but only one survived," said the woman. "Predators took four, and one fell over the weir. I wish they wouldn't swim so close to the weir and nest in such an exposed area."

She rambled on about the current lack of reeds to hide the swans, the inappropriate behaviour of pet owners who let their dogs swim in the lake, and the ignorant people who fed the ducks bread and were entertained by their consequent aggressive manner toward each other. Merlyn listened to the long nature lesson, said goodbye, and continued her walk.

Further along the path, Merlyn saw someone running from the duck family with his young dog. Although the ducklings were teenagers now and were the same size as their parents, the dad persisted in being the sole protector. He would storm out of the pack with nothing more than an open, toothless beak and a few pathetic hisses and gallantly try to frighten off intruders. Ineffectual as it was, it seemed to work on this intruder and his pup.

"You are easily scared off," laughed Merlyn.

"I was saving Hardy's life," said Tom.

"Hardy?" asked Merlyn, looking at the dog. "The love of your life?"

"He's a Brussels griffon," explained Tom.

Merlyn laughed.

Although Hardy was very cute with his squashed nose and Ewok-like facial features, she didn't bother to pat him as she could see that his sensitive, alert eyes were only for his master. It was clearly a two-way love affair.

A male swan reared out of the water and squawked at the teenage ducks getting too close to his babies. Unlike father duck, he made an impressive show, but that was all he had—a good show.

"The missionary from the Friends of Edgars Lake told me that swans mate for life and can die if their mate dies," said Merlyn.

"Of a broken heart," said Tom.

"I guess," said Merlyn. "She also told me that occasionally a dad kicks out his wife, takes another male, and the guys raise the children together."

Tom found that amusing. She knew he would.

As Tom turned for home, he said, "See you at Pity."

"Pity?" asked Merlyn.

"That's what the locals call Pittstop," said Tom.

After a few steps, he turned and said, "I do have a boyfriend. A real one."

"Do you?" said Merlyn.

"Yes," said Tom. "And I am gay."

"Really?" said Merlyn.

Tom pranced off with Hardy at his heels. The father duck, once again, ran for them.

"Wouldn't a mass attack be more effective?" Tom called to the duck. "Isn't it time for your kids to pull their own weight?"

Merlyn could see Tom and Hardy in the distance, swanning about, dodging ducks, until they disappeared over the footbridge.

# DIRTY DANCING

## CHAPTER 15
## DIRTY WORK

M erlyn could hear the cafe music, an old song by Steely Dan—Dirty Work, as she approached a distinctive blue door where the words *Tom & Hardy* had been freshly painted.

"Glad you came to see my new place," said Tom. "Take a seat anywhere."

The room was large for a city cafe and had numerous nooks and crannies. Merlyn picked a quiet corner and gathered some hessian cushions with embroidered motifs of Brussels griffons. She knew that Ben could be there. He worked next door at The State Ballet. No longer a performing dancer, he taught and choreographed.

A large, U-shaped lounge in the far corner held a noisy group of lively people. It was Ben, with about eight young dancers and a few staff members. They were all engrossed in their carry-on, so Merlyn watched them in the way that introspects watch people. They stare with inappropriate single-mindedness until something reminds them that it is not polite to peer at people.

Ben was ruling the roost in his understated, polished way. By his age, he was too good at it to have to exert much effort. He smiled, talked, and touched each person just enough to reassure them that they were important to him. The young ones were easy fodder. Not much more than kids; they needed Ben's support. They had their careers to think about. Besides, people tend to fall in love with those who have much more than they do.

Along the way, Ben learned that warmth and humour were the most successful approach to people. However, if challenged, he could be as feral as any outright power maniac (although he preferred not to do his own dirty work unless he had to).

*It's not bad behaviour*, thought Merlyn. *It's normal. Actually, it's more accomplished than normal. At least Ben has some idea that there might be something more. After all, he loved me.*

Merlyn caught the light bouncing from the small window above her onto her water glass and back into a complex world.

Returning her gaze to the group, she thought, *Who am I to judge any of them? They are all building their worlds, growing their abilities, and forming relationships. How else do people learn but by experience and practice?*

The group was on the move. Tom spoke animatedly to them on their way out. Some of the girls hugged him, and some of the boys whacked his bum. Tom knew how to work them. Ben and Tom shook hands. They could read each other without even trying.

After the group left, Tom walked over to Merlyn and said, "Gotta keep the customers happy."

His face changed to a more serious expression, and he said quietly, "They're not my peeps."

## CHAPTER 16
## BLUE SKIES

J ust as Merlyn gathered her things to leave the cafe, Ben opened the blue door and headed for her.

"Did you see me before?" asked Merlyn.

"Of course," said Ben.

*Why didn't you say hello when you were with the others?* thought Merlyn.

After a second thought, she let it go and patted the chair next to her. Having already decided to oblige, Ben sat down. His eyes and voice were soft.

"How're things?" he asked.

"Everything is fine," said Merlyn. "And you?"

"You know, the same," said Ben. "Busy. People. Problems. Ugh!"

They chatted for a few more minutes before Ben said he needed to return to teaching. Giving each other a kiss, they parted peacefully.

As Merlyn paid for her coffee, Tom asked, "Ex?"

Merlyn looked surprised, and Tom shrugged and said, "I've been in hospitality a long time."

"We were married," said Merlyn. "I suppose we still are."

She opened the door onto a splendid blue sky. It back-dropped the city landscape and danced between all the buildings, old and new, wherever it had space. It brought some sparkle into the hordes on the street, who lifted their gaze a little and walked more lightly.

As Merlyn's eyes were drawn to the magnificent sandstone building that became the home of The State Ballet eighty years ago, she thought about all the dancers who had walked in and out of those doors. So many dreams and aspirations, so much failure and disappointment.

In amongst the momentary glory and inevitable change would always be the unrelenting, ferocious desire to express the soul through the mechanics of a limited body in the hope that it could bring some peace to a painful inner and outer world.

*It does do that*, thought Merlyn. *Maybe it's limited. Maybe it's a lot of work for fleeting imperfection, but along with all the dirty work, there is also love. Along with all the dirty dancing, there is also purity. Along with all the hatred, hurt, and anger, there is also healing. That is the life of a ballet company. Indeed, that is life.*

# REPEAT OR DELETE

# CHAPTER 17
# THE AUDITION

As the students were on holiday, Ben took the rare opportunity to sit alone in Tom & Hardy to look through the recently published *Eighty Years of The State Ballet.*

"You in that?" asked Tom.

"Yep," said Ben, pointing to one of the later pages in the book.

"Impressive," said Tom.

Ben didn't reply.

"Can I have a look?" asked Tom.

He opened it, searched the first few pages, and said, "Found it. That's my grandfather there. He was one of the corps de ballet in the early days. He wasn't really a ballet dancer. He was a self-taught ice skater, but, back then, the company was desperate for male dancers, so they took him."

"Different nowadays," said Ben.

He then thought that might sound rude about Tom's grandfather. He was about to qualify his statement when Tom put up his hand to indicate there was no need.

"Eighty years ago, no one wanted to be seen as gay, but everyone knows male dancers are gay," said Tom with a wink. "It was harder then. To be gay, that is. Not harder to be a male ballet dancer. That was easier."

After a pause, he said, "My grandfather wasn't gay."

Ben laughed and said, "Otherwise, you wouldn't be here, right?"

"When my grandfather was twenty, he saw a sign advertising male ballet auditions. He struggled to make ends meet from skating. So, with no ballet training, he went to the audition. The guys were asked to lift their leg off the ground and hold it for five minutes. Whoever was left standing was in. My grandfather had a great aversion to poverty. That leg was staying up even if it killed him. He probably had an advantage because he was used to holding up heavy skating boots for spirals."

Ben wasn't sure what an ice-skating spiral was, but he guessed it was like a ballet arabesque with an open hip because skaters open their hips out, unlike ballet dancers.

"Skaters don't have nice, pointed, precise feet like ballet dancers," said Tom. "They are used to bulky boots. Their feet don't get to move much."

"How long was he with the company for?" asked Ben, who was quite taken with the story.

"Only a few years," said Tom. "Then he went back to skating, did shows, met my grandmother (a national champion skater), fought to win her over, got married, left skating, got a job in printing, hated it, stayed there anyway, and tried to live his life as best he could with all the problems he had from a dysfunctional upbringing."

"Wow," said Ben, who didn't know why he was so interested in the story, but he was. "Was that the end of ballet and skating in the family?"

"My grandparents' kids skated with some success, including my mother," said Tom. "And my brother and I skated."

"Really?" said Ben.

He wanted to ask if Tom was any good.

"My brother and I are third-generation skaters," said Tom. "We can skate."

Ben looked at Tom's thin, fine body with long, lean muscles.

*A dancer's body*, he thought.

He knew that Tom had fast feet by the way he moved around the tables and customers, balancing plates and avoiding stray toddlers.

"My brother and I both gave up skating years ago," said Tom.

Ben knew that Tom must be doing something to keep his body strong and supple if he was no longer skating.

"Have you been back?" asked Ben.

"Nah," said Tom. "One day, I took my skates off and threw them in the bin, even though they were only two months old and cost me a few thousand dollars. I never wanted to see them again."

Ben sensed that Tom was done with the conversation. Looking around the cafe, he wondered if Tom chose the position because it was next to The State Ballet.

"I'm back here where my grandfather started," said Tom. "I guess we have trouble deleting some things."

Ben gave a philosophical shrug and headed back to the sandstone building with only half his mind on the day's jobs.

## CHAPTER 18
## ONE DANCE

"It's your birthday in a few days," said Ben on the phone to Merlyn, while walking back to work. "What do you want?"

"What's been happening?" asked Merlyn.

"Did you know Tom from next door was a skater?" said Ben.

"No," said Merlyn.

"A third-generation skater. And his grandfather danced with us in the early years."

"Wow," said Merlyn, repeating Ben's sentiment. "There is nothing arty about his cousin here at Pittstop. Skating must come from the other side of the family."

Returning to Ben's original question, Merlyn said, "Since you are offering about my birthday, there is something I'd like."

"Yes?" said Ben.

"I'd like you to teach me how to dance," said Merlyn.

"Don't be ridiculous," said Ben. "I'm not offering that.

Besides, you can't learn ballet now. I barely even do it myself anymore. And I'd be too hard on you. You'd hate it."

Merlyn remembered one of Ben's colleagues saying that one shouldn't be taught by a family member, especially a partner, because they are either too soft or too hard. Merlyn assumed that included, if not emphasised, ex-partners.

"I'll take that risk," said Merlyn. "Just one dance. Teach me one dance."

Ben sighed and said, "Okay, just one. Come this week while the students are away."

Late that evening, Merlyn got a text from Ben, *Tomorrow, 1 pm.*

## CHAPTER 19
## DON'T SIT IN YOUR ARSE

"Stand up. Get your head up. Centre in. Eyes forward. Don't lean on me," commanded Ben. "Don't sit in your arse. Stand on your legs. Use your feet. Point them. You're rounding your shoulders. Centre in. Centre in!"

At one point, he stopped in exasperation and said, "You are dancing like a needy little child. Stand up and get out of my space!"

Merlyn would have objected, but she knew it was all perfectly true. After two hours of repetition, she managed to do a very basic pas de deux with Ben.

"Okay, that's it," said Ben. "Times up. That's more private lesson time than most dancers get."

Merlyn was sweating. Ben wasn't.

"Happy birthday," he added more softly.

He was waiting for a response from Merlyn, who was still catching her breath. After the million commands he had thrown at her, he was fairly sure that her dancing aspirations would have been redirected.

"How did you like it?" he asked finally.

"I loved it," said Merlyn with unashamed exhilaration.

"Oh," said Ben.

"Can we do it again?" asked Merlyn.

"No," said Ben. "Definitely not. I don't teach private lessons except to the soloists and pas de deux couples. I certainly don't teach beginners. Go to an adult ballet class."

Merlyn shook her head.

"Well, get someone else to teach you who does that sort of thing," said Ben.

Again, Merlyn shook her head.

"I can't help you," said Ben, walking towards the door.

"Text me a time," Merlyn called after him.

# PART II
# SILENT ORDER

# JOE-JOE'S APARTMENTS

## CHAPTER 20
## THE DREAM AND
## DOCTOR APOLLO

A few months ago, when Edgars Lake had resigned to winter, and the six cygnets had grown and flown, Merlyn had a lucid dream. It was as real as reality, at least until normal life had a chance to claim the day. It went like this:

Merlyn lived in a female hermitage. The inhabitants wore long gowns, although clothes were neither here nor there because everyone was translucent and shining. Whatever needed to be communicated was done telepathically.

Strange as it sounds, Merlyn spent nearly all her time in one room. Seven years passed in this way.

One would assume that one would get very bored
being stuck in a room with nothing to do for seven
years. Yet, that was far from the case. It was exquis-
itely beautiful, but not in a way that can be explained
in words.

At the end of the dream, Merlyn was told that
although there were no similar places on Earth, there
were many watered-down versions taking numerous
forms.

The dream was not forgotten; could not be forgotten.

MERLYN BEGAN CALLING into a cafe between Pittown and the
city. It was on the ground level of Joe-Joe's Apartments and
bordered the National Botanic Gardens. It wasn't the cafe
that interested Merlyn. It was some of the people in it,
particularly one man.

He was about seventy, the sort of seventy that has benefited from seven decades. He looked normal enough; a bit
balding, a little plump. His accent was European, maybe
Hungarian. His clothes were somewhat formal for ordinary
daywear, perhaps a remnant from a past profession.

Merlyn heard one of the man's companions call him Dr
Apollo. That explained the clothes. His eyes were exceptionally intelligent, kind, and joyful. His presence radiated a
strong sense of peace and quiet power. He sometimes smiled
at Merlyn from where he sat with his friends.

For her part, Merlyn was irresistibly drawn to him.

Students recognise their teachers. Teachers recognise their students.

One afternoon, Merlyn followed Dr Apollo into the apartment lift. She intended to pretend she was visiting someone on one of the floors. The lift passed Level 1 and Level 2, then stopped at the top floor, Level 3. As the door opened, she saw a small, gold sign on the wall opposite: *The Silent Order.*

Being the last floor, it was silly to pretend she was going elsewhere. Resigning herself to the awkwardness of the situation, she took a step forward—one little step.

"Your floor is very quiet," said Merlyn.

*It isn't just a lack of noise,* she thought. *It's something positively present, not merely the absence of something.*

She followed Dr Apollo down the hallway. They came to a communal lounge room with a panoramic view of the city from full-length windows.

"Why does the sign say, *The Silent Order?*" asked Merlyn.

"We, on this floor," said Dr Apollo, "live here in order to develop our inner silence. Everyone is free to come and go. They go to work, do activities, and see friends and family. However, we all return to the silence. The silence is constant. The noise is temporary."

## CHAPTER 21
## GOODBYE

I n Joe-Joe's Apartments:
After living in Pittown for a year, Merlyn moved into Level 3 of Joe-Joe's Apartments. From her balcony, the city view was not as extensive as the view from the communal sitting room, but she could see the Botanic Gardens from her side of the building. A pathway leading to a large rock was particularly interesting. The flat-topped rock looked perfect for sitting. A circular stone wall protected the area, which was roofed by a rainforest canopy.

Turning her attention to the city skyline, Merlyn's eyes rested on the State Ballet building where Ben worked. She then thought about Tom's cafe next door to it. Her last visit there was six months ago.

~

SIX MONTHS AGO, *in Tom & Hardy:*
On entering the distinctive blue door of Tom & Hardy, Merlyn noticed that Tom looked strained and withdrawn.

He seemed to be avoiding her. However, he seemed to be avoiding everyone while still carrying out his regular duties. Eventually, he had to serve her as no one else came. He tried to escape after Merlyn's order was taken, but she put her hand on his arm.

"Wait," said Merlyn. "What's the matter?"

"Nothing," said Tom, trying to wriggle away.

"Please," said Merlyn, "talk to me."

With resignation, Tom sat down and said quietly, "I'm leaving."

"What do you mean 'leaving'? Are you selling?" asked Merlyn.

"No," said Tom. "I'm keeping the business, but I'm not working in it anymore. I'll manage it from a distance with short visits to keep it functioning properly. I'll probably open some more places and do the same there."

"Don't say anything," he added. "No one knows."

Merlyn looked around the cafe. She wondered if the new direction would work from a business point of view, but Tom was very experienced in hospitality.

"Don't people come here because of you?" asked Merlyn.

Regardless of her lack of hospitality knowledge, she knew that Tom drew his customers by who he was. Even the staff members were different when he was around. Without him, emptiness stodgily hung in the air.

"Of course, it will work," said Tom confidently. "People do it all the time."

"Oh," said Merlyn. "Do they? Okay."

"I can't stand it," said Tom.

"What can't you stand?" asked Merlyn.

"People," said Tom with barely concealed disgust.

Merlyn hoped that "people" didn't include her. She

didn't think so. The conversation seemed far from over to Merlyn, but Tom returned to serving. Presently, she stood up to leave. What was she going to say to him? She might not see him again. Apart from work, he was basically uncontactable. He purposely wasn't on social media. He didn't give his number out. Merlyn recalled a conversation she overheard when he was doing a shift in Pittstop.

*IN PITTSTOP:*

"Hey, Tom, you are here today," said a youngish, outgoing woman in Pittstop. "I haven't seen you for ages."

She hadn't seen him for ages because, unknown to her, he was opening his own cafe, *Tom & Hardy.*

"I was going to message you but realised I didn't have your number," she added.

She waited for the forthcoming number. That was as likely as a snowball's chance in hell. Tom laughed and returned to the counter.

*BACK IN TOM & Hardy:*

On that last day of seeing Tom, Merlyn walked towards the cash register in Tom & Hardy. Noticing her approach, he disappeared into the kitchen.

*He doesn't want to say goodbye,* she thought sadly.

Say it or not, it was still goodbye.

## CHAPTER 22
## WITHDRAWAL

I t was Merlyn's first community meeting of the Silent Order. She sat on one of the soft, spotlessly white sofas lining the wall of the communal lounge room. The city lights shone through the dark glass.

She recognised some of the eight people from Joe-Joe's cafe below. They weren't like the ethereal people in her dream. They were a mixture of gender, race, appearance, personality, and, as soon became apparent, spiritual development. Dr Apollo loved them all equally as one would love one's children.

Everyone sat quietly with open eyes for about ten minutes, and then Dr Apollo spoke.

"As spiritual students," said Dr Apollo, "we cultivate inner stillness through contemplation or awareness. Behind the normal goings-on of everyday life, we try to have consistent wakefulness. We learn to watch what we are thinking, what other people are thinking, and the spiritual truth of any situation. We live in two realms. One is the visible human realm. The other is the invisible spiritual realm. This is not obvious to anyone except those who do the same thing. Then, it is instantly recognisable."

He smiled at each member to acknowledge the spirit he could see clearly in his Silent Order people.

"Is withdrawal from mainstream life a necessary choice on the spiritual path?" one of the attendees asked. "Is it something everyone should try to do at some point along the way?"

"Withdrawal is not really a choice," said Dr Apollo. "Nor is it something one should try to do. Some people will find that their attachment to the world has, without effort, diminished, and they will crave solitude. They may withdraw from mainstream life to focus on their growth. Withdrawal can be deceptive in appearance. A person can live an apparently solitary lifestyle, but their mind is full of noise. On the other hand, someone can have the appearance of a normal life but, unknown to others, be in a state of inner solitude."

Everyone sat quietly for a further ten minutes.

"Without silence," Dr Apollo concluded the evening, "we can neither know ourselves, another, nor the depth of anything beautiful. Here, in the Silent Order, we learn to take silence into the noise. Good evening, friends."

Back in her apartment, Merlyn's thoughts returned to Tom. *Perhaps "withdrawal" is what Tom is doing, but he can't put it into words. We are all different and conceptualise life differently, but we are probably all seeking the same thing.*

Her worry about his well-being noticeably lessened, and she felt assured that his path was being directed by the same force that nurtured her own.

# STORE CREEK

## CHAPTER 23
## BIRTHDAY BALLET

"Wow," said Ben. "That's a surprise."

Merlyn was pleased. It was a surprise that was a year in the making.

After last year's birthday ballet lesson, Ben never did text Merlyn another lesson time as she had requested. A few reminders and some disappointment later, Merlyn pulled herself together with the thought that if she wanted to dance, it was unrealistic, unfair, and burdensome to expect Ben to facilitate her wishes.

So, she embarked on a training and education regimen that she consistently stuck to throughout the interim year.

As Ben originally suggested, she went to adult ballet classes. She even advanced from the beginner class to the intermediate class. She had private lessons with appropriate teachers who took beginners. She added daily walks, a weekly yoga lesson, and plenty of home stretching to her four-day-a-week dance program. Her fitness, strength, and flexibility improved out of this world.

Mind you, her body hurt every single day. Usually, it was

simple muscle soreness. Sometimes, it was injury. However, each injury taught her something important about what not to do in dancing.

By the end of the year, as she opened the large glass doors of the sandstone ballet building, she realised that she was beginning to vaguely feel like a dancer.

She recalled her catch-ups with Ben over the past twelve months as she walked through the empty corridors, normally full of talkative, energetic dancers (now on holiday). She had seen him about once a month. He had noticed that she was thinner and had more muscle tone, but it didn't cross his mind that she would have embarked on a dance training program without him. Not that he minded. He was rather impressed with the effort and self-reliance that it took.

For Merlyn's part, what she enjoyed most about this year's lesson was a fleeting moment of relaxation in Ben's eyes. Instead of having to carry her for the entire dance, he could, here and there, leave her to do her part and concentrate on his own. It was fleeting, but it was there—a wisp of something new and alive. He could not have known how much that meant to Merlyn.

What is dancing other than the desire for a moment of freely given joint creation? It takes time, but even more than time, it takes trust. Trust, not so much in another (humans are so damn changeable), but trust in the part of another that does not change. The part that is whole and happy.

As Merlyn gathered her things to leave, Ben said unexpectedly, "I also have a surprise for you."

"Really?" said Merlyn. "What is it?"

"I bought a house," said Ben. "Not here in the city. Remember when my grandmother died earlier this year and left the eight grandchildren her house in Store Creek to be equally divided?"

"Yes?" said Merlyn.

"I decided to buy the others out," said Ben.

Getting the seven cousins to agree to sell their part was quite a feat, but eventually, they did. Some needed the money. Some were practical and realised that a part-share in a country house with seven other families would be a disaster in time management. Some were kind and remembered that Ben was the only grandchild who lived there. Due to his family circumstances, he spent much of his primary school years in Store Creek with his grandmother. However, once he reached secondary school and his ballet training became serious, he needed to stay in the city.

"Come, see it," said Ben. "After Christmas, in the January holidays. The garden is gorgeous."

*Garden?* thought Merlyn. *Since when did Ben care about a garden?*

"Meet you at the General Store," said Ben. "You can't miss it."

# CHAPTER 24
# STORE CREEK
# GENERAL STORE

A s Ben said, one couldn't miss Store Creek General Store. It was the only shop in the tiny town. Less than two hours from the city, Store Creek huddled in green, hilly hinterland (yellowish hills in the drier seasons). The General Store lived alongside an old church, the quaint primary school, a dozen houses, and several unused buildings from businesses long since gone. No one needed a blacksmith or stables anymore. At its height, the stables fed ninety horses a day and housed forty-five at night.

Merlyn parked next to a row of thirty motorbikes. She was early. Ben wasn't there yet. Sitting on the veranda, she watched the bikies who had taken over the entire outside area next to the vegetable patch. Mostly grey heads with a few younger ones in between; a motley-looking but well-mannered group. She gathered that this was their regular breakfast spot on their trips from the city. The store owner knew them by name and thanked them for carrying their cups and plates back to the kitchen. Merlyn overheard them talking about one of their recent, self-appointed assignments —protecting a mother and her children from domestic violence. Apparently, they took turns parking conspicuously outside her house.

*I wouldn't like to be that man if he turned up,* thought Merlyn. *He probably didn't. Abusive men aren't brave. It's much more effective than "We can't do anything until something has happened." Any poor woman and her kids could be dead by the time "something" has happened.*

Turning to the wall next to her retro table, Merlyn read about the history of Store Creek. It was unclear whether the town's name came first and the store's second, or whether the town got its name from the store. The latter was a general store in the authentic rural tradition of being a post office, news agency, bank, grocer, and tea room. Nowadays, it was also a semi-reliable wi-fi source in an area with limited and intermittent reception.

Beginning a hundred and fifty years ago, holidaymakers took horse and coach from the last country train station and stopped at Store Creek for horses to be changed and people to be fed. It was three hours through grazing country to Store Creek by coach and then another three hours through the forest to their beachside destination.

The people rode with mailbags, which were lifeblood at the time. The coaches were smaller in winter, with three horses pulling ten people. In summer, that number jumped to six horses and twenty-five people. The dirt roads were muddy and slippery in wet weather. Sometimes, the passengers had to get out and push. Even in dry weather, some slopes were so steep that the driver held the passengers' lives in his hands.

Despite the ups and downs of the trip (or because of

them), the views were magnificent to behold. It was a great delight for tired, dusty people and horses to cool down in the ocean at the journey's end. That six-hour coach journey now takes forty minutes. Regardless, Store Creek General Store kept its appeal.

## CHAPTER 25
## NANNA'S HOUSE

"Y ou still have your grandmother's sign on the gate," said Merlyn as she pointed to it—*Nanna's House.*

"Yeah, I know," said Ben. "I keep thinking I'll take it off, but then I can't bring myself to do it."

*There is probably a bit more "Nanna" in Ben,* thought Merlyn, *than he would want to know about anyway.*

The house was delightful—an unadulterated 1950's house with furniture to match. It even had an old tube television.

"You have to get up to change channels," said Ben with some annoyance.

He watched it at night because his phone reception was so bad that he mostly had no internet. It took him a while to get used to the tank water. It tasted delicious, but showers had to be very short and flushing the toilet was a hit-or-miss venture because the water pressure was so low. The feature of the house was the garden. It was completely overgrown with an incredible array of plants, all growing beautifully and fighting for space. The fruit trees were covered with fruit. The flowers were glorious.

"Lucky, here in this pocket, it rains enough to keep the garden going," said Ben.

"Are you going to garden?" asked Merlyn.

"As if!" said Ben. "It'll look after itself, and when it gets bad enough, I'll get someone to help."

A few happy hours later, Ben suggested, "Next time you visit, stay the night."

Merlyn looked at him, but he turned away and added awkwardly, "'Cause, you know, there's room... spare rooms."

"Sure," said Merlyn. "I'll help you with the garden."

She looked out into the wild mess of fruit and flowers, full of summer life force, and said, "We can all use a little help, right?"

# LOVERS, FAIRIES,
# AND FOOLS

# CHAPTER 26
# MIDSUMMER'S DREAM

D r Apollo sat on the middle rock in the Botanic Gardens meditation area as if it had been put there especially for him. The Silent Order had its meetings there during the summer.

Nearby, a theatre company that performed regular productions of *Shakespeare in the Gardens* was beginning *A Midsummer Night's Dream*. The breeze intermittently carried the actors' voices into the fern gully, where Merlyn and the small group listened attentively to their teacher.

"Ladies and gentlemen," announced the commentator, "this evening, we have the pleasure of bringing you the jewel of Shakespeare's comedies, *A Midsummer Night's Dream*. Come to a magical world of lovers, fairies, and fools."

"Lovers, fairies, and fools," repeated Dr Apollo. "We are all cast in this play and alternate between characters until we tire of it and retire from acting."

He listened to the noises around him—passing people, birds in their climactic finale of the day, distant traffic, the silent talk of the trees, the secret sounds of the energetic world vibrating with meaningful rhythm. Dr Apollo listened consciously. He also spoke consciously. One had the impression that every word was sent forth into the world as an entity unto itself.

Turning to one of his more pretentious students, he asked, "Alexander, which are you? Lover, fairy, or fool?"

Everyone laughed—except Alexander, who had taken offence and was preparing a comeback. About the same age as Dr Apollo, Alexander had had a high-flying professional career and was well-educated in psychology and spirituality. He often tried to assume the role of auxiliary teacher. However, his attempts to do so met with much eye-rolling as he markedly lacked the willingness to practise what he preached. His life was a series of relationship breakdowns and problems of every kind. Alexander's defensiveness merely added to the comical nature of the situation.

Over the past few months, Merlyn noticed that Dr Apollo often pointed out his students' shortcomings in front of others. He didn't do it to hurt them but to help them. He said that embarrassment, although uncomfortable, was a necessary precursor to recognising one's mistakes and making progress on the path. Speaking openly about another's faults in a well-intentioned, direct manner is often humorous because we all tend to know the truth about people, even though it is usually not mentioned outright.

*Human nature is ridiculous,* thought Merlyn. *Ridiculous and stupid.*

## CHAPTER 27
## WHAT ABOUT ME?

"The course of true love never did run smooth," was heard from the theatre group as the four young Athenian characters of the play became more deeply entrenched in their problematic relationships.

"What is love?" asked Dr Apollo.

"Not you, Alexander," he added.

Again, to Alexander's annoyance, everyone laughed. He was the only one who couldn't see the joke. Half an hour passed, and various students gave their opinions on love. Most were boring. There were a few touching moments when someone inadvertently shared a moment of rawness from their lives.

*As far as people go,* thought Merlyn, *this is a well-functioning group of humans, above average in intelligence, care, and awareness. Yet, everyone is in pain.*

Deciding it was time to end the discussion about love, Dr Apollo said, "Most of our problems would be gone if we stopped saying three little words. Does anyone know what they are?"

Some of the students offered suggestions.

"What. About. Me?" said Dr Apollo. "What about me? If we stopped asking this question, 90% of our problems would disappear."

Puck, one of the fairies of A *Midsummer Night's Dream,* concluded the play,

*If we shadows have offended,*
*Think but this, and all is mended,*
*That you have but slumber'd here*
*While these visions did appear.*
*And this weak and idle theme,*
*No more yielding but a dream.*

"You have but slumbered here," said Dr Apollo.

He looked into the rainforest canopy and watched the fading light flicker through the soft green.

"Night is approaching," he said. "Time to go home."

# HIDDEN ENTRANCE

## CHAPTER 28
## ELEMENTS OF LIFE

I *n Store Creek:*

It was only the first month of autumn, but the mornings in Store Creek were already cold. Ben's grandmother's house was not climate-controlled like his city apartment, where inside living was so monotone that you couldn't even tell the outside temperature. In *Nanna's House,* there were holes everywhere—between the floorboards, around the windows, and, essentially, wherever there was a join of some sort. Ben thought there were so many holes in the house that he practically lived outside.

Heating depended on the old wood burner in the centre of the lounge room. Although it was the same burner as when Ben lived there as a child, he had no idea how it worked. He tried starting it, but it wouldn't fire up properly. When he opened the burner's door to check on its slow progress, it spewed smoke into the room. He shut the door, gave up on his fire-making ability, and put on a coat.

The next morning, feeling the cold seep into his bones, he gave the fire another attempt. He stared at it and told both himself and the burner that he was not incompetent and could surely work it out.

*Instructions?* he thought.

He found a faint label on the back of the burner that read:

*Air is food for fire. To get the fire going, the flue needs to be wide open. Once the fire is cranking along, close the flue, or your wood will disappear before your eyes, and all the heat will travel up the flue and out into the world.*
*However, when it is time to add more wood to your fire, open the flue again, or your cosy lounge room will become a smoke-filled, cosy lounge room.*

*Great,* thought Ben. *Open the flue. Flue, where are you? What does a flue look like?*

He found a knob at the back of the burner.

*It moves,* he thought. *It must be the flue.*

He triumphantly opened it to start the fire. Once the fire was roaring, he closed it again and watched with fascination as the burner slowly ate through the wood while sending out a massive amount of beautiful heat.

## CHAPTER 29
## PEARS, PEACHES, AND PLUMS

B en didn't come to Store Creek as often as he thought he would. Like most holiday house owners, he had intended to come every weekend. However, it took a big effort to extricate himself from life and work in the city. Besides, the quietness of Store Creek was a little unsettling. It was fantastic for a little while, but quickly became disconcerting. Most people cannot tolerate peace and quiet for too long. The typical life cycle of a holiday house is to be visited with great excitement for a little while and then abandoned for most of the year.

What's more, although Ben originally wanted many visitors, he found that, after a while, he didn't. There was something about the house that brought out Ben's deeper side. He wondered if it was because it was the place of his childhood, or if it was the effect of being in such a tiny town, or if it was because something was happening to him. Perhaps the house was an auxiliary to that rather than an initiator.

Pears, peaches, and plums littered the pathway where

Ben walked. He pulled a handful of grapes from the archway.

*Delicious,* he thought. *Nothing tastes like homegrown fruit.*

He remembered a story that Merlyn once told him about a rural community in Russia where everyone grew their food on their small patches of land. That was not so unusual, but in this community, the gardens grew their produce in a way that most benefited the particular physical needs of the individual owners. As a result, illness was rare. No one could explain it. If they could, they weren't saying anything.

Along with the rest of the garden, the vine over the front door at Nanna's House had been given free rein and completely covered the entranceway. If you didn't know where the door was, you wouldn't easily find it. Ben liked it like that. The vine swayed in the breeze, allowing Ben to enter. Going inside the cottage was like entering his inner world—private and unfathomable.

# RETURN OF
# THE WARRIORS

## CHAPTER 30
## GYM GURU

*In Waldmeer, at the Waldmeer Warriors:*

When Ben was at Store Creek, he often drove to the gym in the nearby seaside village of Waldmeer. Being an ex-dancer, he looked after his body. Pulling up at the gym this morning, he looked at the ageing sign, *Waldmeer Warriors.*

The gym owner, Malik, not long ago, told Ben that he had owned it for nearly twenty years. He was in his mid-forties. The business was a family affair. Malik's wife, Rachael, was usually at the desk, and their three kids were generally not far away. The oldest of them, Michael, who was nineteen, had taken a shine to Ben. Most people liked Ben.

"You're here," said Michael excitedly. "I'll work with you."

Michael was a great talker, although some things, even for him, were off-limits. Today, those boundaries became a touch blurred.

"My Dad named me after his first-ever client," said Michael. "When he came to Waldmeer, he trained a shy, skinny kid from the local area who now owns a fitness empire."

Ben raised his eyebrows.

"The empire is not here in Waldmeer," said Michael. "My namesake says that this is Dad's territory. He always talks about his 'guru' (my Dad) in his training programs, but he never mentions Dad's name because he knows that Dad doesn't want people coming to him for the wrong reasons."

Ben had noticed Michael's little sister on previous occasions. The thirteen-year-old girl was not particularly noticeable, as she was a quiet little thing. However, he saw how protective Malik was of her.

"Who is your little sister named after?" asked Ben.

"My grandmother, Faith-Amira," replied Michael.

"Your sister's name is Faith-Amira?" asked Ben.

"No," said Michael. "Her name is Maria."

Michael shrugged.

"I don't know why she's called Maria if she's supposed to be named after my grandmother, but that's how it is."

Michael didn't overthink things. Unlike his little sister, he accepted life as it presented itself.

"My Dad says that Maria has my grandmother's eyes."

"Where is your grandmother?" asked Ben.

"Oh, we have never met her," replied Michael. "She left a year before I was born."

Ben assumed she had died.

"She didn't die," said Michael. "She just went somewhere and didn't come back. She had a friend called Gabriel who apparently went to be with my grandmother and also never returned."

"Not your grandfather?" queried Ben.

"No, my grandfather is Papa Zufar," said Michael. "We

have never met him either. Dad says he's a fly-by-night sort of guy."

After a pause, Michael added wistfully, "Sometimes, I think Dad is sad because he can't see his mother, and I guess he would like his family to know us kids."

"Excuse me. You might want to move your car," said a soft, sweet voice behind Ben.

Turning around, Ben looked down to see Maria.

"The parking patrolman is coming," she said.

Ben walked to his car. Indeed, at the far end of the street, the parking officer was slowly making his way down the block. Returning to Michael, Ben asked how Maria knew the parking officer was coming, as she had been sitting near her father the entire time.

"She knows stuff like that," said Michael.

"Like lotto numbers?" asked Ben, only half-joking.

"No," said Michael offhandedly. "She doesn't do that."

Michael suddenly felt his father's gaze upon him, and he said abruptly, "See ya later."

## CHAPTER 31
## TURN ON YOUR HEART

I n *Wurt Wurt Koort:*

After the gym, Ben often stopped in Wurt Wurt Koort, the town between Waldmeer and Store Creek, which was at the highest point along the forest road.

"How are you today, bud?" asked Rybert as Ben walked into Wurt Wurt Koort Tearooms.

Rybert was about sixty and told Ben earlier that he had owned the cafe for decades. He was always fun to talk to. In the backroom, his favourite Richard Simmonds program was playing. Seeing Ben's reaction to the flamboyant exercise phenomenon of decades past, Rybert started singing along loudly with exaggerated sincerity, "Turn on your heart. Turn it on for you and me."

"Hi, Ben," said another familiar voice.

"Tom!" said Ben. "What are you doing here? We haven't seen you at Tom & Hardy for a year. Do you still own it?"

Tom's little Brussels griffon followed his master closely.

"Yep, I do," said Tom. "I've been there, but you haven't seen me."

"He's been spending a lot of time here with me in Wurt Wurt Koort," said Rybert affectionately of his younger friend. "We love having him. We want to keep him."

"I'm having a sabbatical," said Tom.

"A year is a long sabbatical," said Ben sarcastically.

Tom shrugged. He didn't care what other people thought about his life.

Looking back at Rybert, Ben asked, "Do you know the family who owns the Waldmeer Warriors?"

"Malik? Yeah, dude. I know him," answered Rybert.

"Why?" he added cautiously.

Ben caught Rybert's expression and pursued the conversation hopefully. "I spoke to Malik's son, Michael, this morning, and he said...."

Rybert interrupted. "Don't mind, Michael. He blabs on."

After a pause, Rybert said, "I knew Michael's grandmother a long time ago."

"Yes?" said Ben. "Nannie Faith-Amira? Is that her name?"

Rybert laughed. "I suppose, by now, she would be seventy and well and truly nannie-material with four grandchildren I know of. When I knew her, she only had one—a spirited kid called Lentilly. We all called her Lentil."

He laughed at the memory and said, "She hated it. In those days, their family was brand new to Waldmeer."

He added as an afterthought, "Faith wasn't a normal nannie."

"Malik has siblings?" asked Ben, who was more interested in Malik's generation (being his own) than before or after.

"An older sister called Bethany and a younger brother called Aristotle," said Rybert. "Bethany is Lentilly's mother, and I don't know if Aristotle has children."

"Where are they now?" asked Ben.

Rybert's face changed expression, and Ben could tell he was shutting down the conversation.

"Malik is the only member of his family in these parts," said Rybert.

He turned to go back to work.

Ben couldn't help asking one more question. "What about the guy who followed Faith-Amira? Gabriel was his name, I think."

Rybert stopped walking and turned back to face Ben.

"I knew him, too," said Rybert.

"Yes?" said Ben encouragingly.

Rybert stared out the cafe window into the main street of Wurt Wurt Koort. These days, the town was doing nicely. Very few witches were left. His mother had passed on ten years ago. There wasn't even a proper coven of thirteen witches anymore. He didn't bother to answer Ben's question.

Tom was as much in the dark as Ben was. They both looked at each other and shook their heads as if to say, *Old people. What can you do? Thank God it's not us!*

## CHAPTER 32
## TIME TO GO HOME

*In Joe-Joe's Apartments:*

Back in Merlyn's apartment building, she and the other Silent Order students were commiserating that Dr Apollo couldn't lead the regular community meeting. He was having a minor procedure at the hospital. A couple who had been with him as students for the last twenty years drove him in. They were waiting for the doctor's okay before ringing about his progress.

When the phone rang, the students were so busy with their conversations that they took little notice. However, a deathly silence fell on the group as the recipient of the call informed everyone that their teacher had passed on in the operation due to anaesthetic issues. They all sat there in disbelief until everyone eventually went to bed, although there was almost no sleep on Level 3 that evening.

Merlyn recalled that lately, Dr Apollo had been ending his meetings with the exact words that he had ended one of the summer meetings in the National Botanic Gardens.

You have but slumbered here.
Night is approaching.
Time to go home.

# CHAPTER 33
# SPIRIT LIFTING

I*n Store Creek:*
Having had little sleep for a week, Merlyn went for a drive to Store Creek in the hope that the countryside would lift her spirits. At Store Creek General Store, she overheard the owner say that he needed temporary staff as he and his wife were going on an extended holiday during the quieter autumn and winter months. His wife wasn't well, and they had decided to do more of the things they enjoyed.

*Good decision,* thought Merlyn.

She then made her own decision on a sudden but definite idea. Ten minutes later, she rang Ben.

"What's up?" Ben said in the distinctive way men can answer the phone, indicating they are available for purpose-oriented conversation only.

"I'm in Store Creek," said Merlyn. "I came for a drive because the community leader at the apartments died last week."

"Sorry," said Ben.

Merlyn wasn't looking for a shoulder to cry on (not that it was being offered).

"I'm going to do some part-time work at Store Creek General Store," said Merlyn. "I need somewhere to live. Can I rent your house until I find somewhere else?"

It was true that Ben was surprised, but he was already used to Merlyn doing surprising things. Now and again, it was as if someone told her a new plan, and that was that.

Ben was due to teach his next ballet class, so he quickly said, "Okay, yes. I haven't been there much lately, anyway."

"Great," said Merlyn. "I'll fix the garden up for you. When I passed your house earlier on, I could see that the vine on the front door is so overgrown that it's a wonder you can even find the way in."

Merlyn was about to hang up when Ben said, "Guess who I met at the cafe in that little town halfway to Waldmeer?"

"No idea," said Merlyn. "I've never been there."

"Tom from Tom & Hardy," said Ben.

"Really?" said Merlyn. "I'll stop there in case he is still around."

"It's worth a visit," said Ben. "You will like it there. Also…"

He wanted to tell her about Malik's family at the Waldmeer Warriors because, for some reason, he couldn't get them out of his mind. However, he didn't know how to relay the story without sounding foolish.

"By the way," he said, "they have dance aerobic classes at the gym in Waldmeer if you're interested."

He knew that if she went to the gym, she would realise there was something unusual about the place.

And so, after six months in the Silent Order at Joe-Joe's

Apartments, Merlyn moved to Store Creek. She wasn't exactly leaving the Silent Order because one cannot really leave such a thing. It would always remain inside her, growing in its own particular way over the years.

Although Merlyn naturally assumed that Store Creek was the important place for her to be, she did not realise that Store Creek was predominantly a gateway. She was entering the mysterious world of Waldmeer, a world of incredible energetic diversity and history.

# PART III
# BACK TO THE BORDER

# THE BORDER

## CHAPTER 34
## TWENTY YEARS

C*ypress Lane in Waldmeer:*
          "It's taken me twenty years to get back here," said Rybert as he walked up and down Cypress Lane.

"Twenty fucking years," he complained as if it had to be someone's fault.

A few days ago, after speaking with Ben about Faith, Rybert told himself that he was going to finish off what he had started. What he had started, he wasn't quite sure.

T*WENTY* *YEARS* *AGO, in the inter-dimensional Borderfirma Lowlands:*

Twenty years ago, Rybert's Aunt Charity told him that she had seen the gathering of two armies in her crystal ball (the sister ball to Nina's of the Great Valley in the Border-firma Mountains). She also told him to go to the battle and that the ball didn't make mistakes. He was to get there via the lane of cypress trees, which ran along the beachfront in Waldmeer.

Once Rybert arrived in the inter-dimensional land of the Borderfirma Lowlands, he only stayed with Faith in Floating Cave Monastery for two nights because she sent him back.

Returning to his life in Wurt Wurt Koort, he was, frankly, angry. Didn't Faith appreciate the courage it took to venture somewhere he had never been? Besides, even though she also sent Gabriel back, he was fairly sure she let some people stay with her. Why? Why not him?

Further, a few months after he and Gabriel returned to Earth, Gabriel disappeared, never to be seen again. Rybert knew that he must have gone back to Borderfirma.

*Well, she didn't send him back again,* he muttered.

He knew the whole thing sounded childish, but Rybert wasn't one to lie to himself. He couldn't see the point in doing that.

Back to now in *Cypress Lane:*

As he wandered along Cypress Lane, he wondered if his attempt to return to Borderfirma was a finishing or a start-ing. Either way, it seemed to him the way forward. A problem that he didn't foresee was that he couldn't make Cypress Lane work as a gateway. He tried a few different evenings, but nothing happened. He had already arranged for Tom and Merlyn to take his shifts in the tearooms. As he kept returning home to the cafe, they asked him why he hadn't gone yet.

"I don't know!" he grumped at them, indicating he didn't wish to discuss the topic.

Merlyn and Tom decided to leave him alone.

One morning, he was nowhere to be found, and they assumed he had finally gone on his holiday or wherever he was going.

Rybert eventually worked out that Cypress Lane only worked as a portal if one cooperated. *Cooperating* meant that one had to calm one's mind and be willing to be taken wherever the gateway deemed appropriate. He must have released himself to its power because, without fanfare, he felt himself being transported to a different world.

## CHAPTER 35
## WATER UNDER THE BRIDGE

I n Waldmeer, at the Waldmeer Warriors:

Although Merlyn decided to do the dance aerobics class at the Waldmeer Warriors as Ben had suggested, it wasn't Malik and his family that caught her attention. She stood in front of the full-length mirror at the gym and started stretching before the class. A kind-looking woman with long grey hair and bright, hippy-type leggings stood beside her.

"Mind if I join you?" asked the woman. "These days, if I don't warm up properly, I pay for it."

"Sure," said Merlyn, making space in front of the limited mirror area.

"I'm Ide," said the woman holding her hand out to Merlyn.

"Nice to meet you," said Merlyn, who already liked the woman more than one tends to like strangers.

"I'm Merlyn. Does the class move fast?"

"I'm not sure," said Ide. "It's my first time here. But, knowing Farkas, I imagine he will make us work."

"Is he the teacher?" asked Merlyn.

"Yes," said Ide. "He's my long-time friend and convinced me to come along."

Ide slowly and systematically moved all her limbs.

"My partner, Salt, died a few months ago," said Ide, "and Farkas thought I needed something to bring me back to life, so he suggested I come."

"Oh, I'm so sorry," said Merlyn.

Glancing at Ide's face (which looked about sixty), Merlyn added, "It's hard to lose someone when they aren't that...."

She searched for the right word as she didn't want to say *old*.

Catching her drift, Ide said accommodatingly, "Oh, he was old."

She laughed good-naturedly and said, "He was ninety."

The conversation stopped for a while as Merlyn processed that information.

Seeing the soft and deep look in Merlyn's eyes, Ide said, "The thing is, Merlyn, we were friends. For two decades, I had a real friend. A wonderful friend. He was a wonderful man. Well known in these parts and also in the hills."

She pointed to the back hills of Waldmeer, where some of Salt's relatives, the Clinkers, lived.

Farkas strode confidently into the room. He was probably about seventy, but Merlyn felt that it would be foolish to be lulled into a false sense of complacency.

Looking directly at Ide, Farkas said, "Welcome, everyone. It's good to see you."

He then glanced around the room to include anyone who wanted to be included. If they didn't want to be, he didn't look like he cared.

Although Ide and Farkas both lived in Waldmeer for all

the years that Ide and Salt were together, Ide and Farkas's contact had been minimal for the past ten years or so. Their son, Lan-Lan, was now in his early twenties and lived overseas. A lot of water had passed under the bridge for all of them.

Recently, Farkas told himself that it was way too much water to fuss about, and that is how he came to contact Ide and suggest she come to his classes. He didn't want her to grieve for too long and knew that Salt was a damn fine man. Ide would be missing him acutely.

Today, Ide and Farkas were simply grateful for a lovely Waldmeer morning, that they were alive and could freely move, and that their son (whom they both adored) was doing well in life.

# CHAPTER 36
# ANCIENT BELL

I n the inter-dimensional *Borderfirma Lowlands:*
As soon as Rybert materialised in the inter-dimensional Borderfirma Lowlands, he breathed a relieved sigh. He recognised the ancient bell and its vibrating announcement of a visitor. He glanced expectantly towards the weathered, green door of Floating Cave Monastery. He could smell the salt from the pond in the cave behind him.

*I never did like that cave,* he thought.

His thoughts were interrupted by a monk opening the Monastery door, who looked as ancient as the bell.

"Come in," said the monk with the sort of calm eyes that belong to eternity.

"I knew you were coming," said the monk, "but I didn't know when. Come in and have some tea. Do you remember the way to the kitchen?"

*Second on the left,* Rybert recalled. He remembered having tea there with Faith on his last visit.

While boiling the kettle, the monk explained, "I'm the

only one here now. Not that I mind. People like us can't feel alone."

He seemed to be including Rybert in the "us", but Rybert thought he was quite capable of feeling alone. Although, come to think about it, he did have an unusually high tolerance for being happy with his own company.

"I was one of the original Floating Cave Monastery monks who had to flee when Evanora took control of the Lowlands," said the monk. "Lady Pearl allowed me to reside in her land, but when Lady Faith asked for the best mystics of each land to congregate at the Monastery here, Lady Pearl did not hesitate in sending me back."

He relayed the story without a trace of pride. He was just stating how it was.

"The others have all gone now except, of course, for Aristotle and his guardian, Odin."

"Where is Aristotle?" asked Rybert.

"He and Indra have been running the Borderfirma Lowlands since they were twenty," said the monk. "Let's see. That must be thirteen years ago now. They share the same birthday, you know."

The monk said this as if Rybert would surely know such a thing, but Rybert had never met Indra. Faith had told him that Indra's father, Peter, who helped her at the monastery, was the best snake-catcher of the Lowlands and came from a hidden line of Lowland mystics.

*I guess they wouldn't be hidden anymore,* thought Rybert, *if Aristotle and Indra are calling the shots.*

"Would you like Peter to take you to Aristotle and Indra?" asked the monk, pointing next door to the cottage where Peter still lived.

Rybert hesitated, and the monk said, "Perhaps, you would prefer to see Lady Faith? She is visiting Odin in the Great Valley because his mother, Nina, recently passed on. Peter will take you there tomorrow morning."

## CHAPTER 37
## DEJA VU

In the *Borderfirma Mountains:*
The following day, when Rybert arrived at Odin's cottage, the excitement of meeting with Faith after so long was overshadowed by another excitement.

"You have opened the gateway!" said Faith animatedly to Rybert. "After you and Gabriel returned to Earth via the bell, it only worked once more."

Rybert guessed that the last time it worked was when Gabriel used it to get back to Borderfirma. He looked around, but there was no sign of Gabriel, and he didn't want to bring him up.

"After that, it didn't work again," said Faith. "Until now."

Everyone looked at Rybert admiringly, which only made him feel silly because he knew nothing about any of it. Further, he was concerned that it seemed to have consequences that everyone was in on except him.

Seeing his expression, Faith said, "It means we can travel again. I can go back to Waldmeer."

"But I have only just arrived," said Rybert.

*I don't know why the Round-Earthers insist on calling her Faith, not Lady Faith,* Odin thought disgruntledly. *Most of the time, Gabriel doesn't even call her Faith. He calls her Amira.*

"I don't want to go back," continued Rybert. "I wouldn't have come if I weren't intending to stay."

As he said the words, he had a strong sense of deja vu. Faith smiled lovingly and looked at his face. He had aged well for an Earth-dweller. The same boyish face with a few more lines. Rybert relaxed and looked around to see a number of Odin's young warriors in the background.

"Oooh, I like a man in uniform," he said.

Although Faith laughed, Rybert was clearly not endearing himself to Odin, who rolled his eyes and started walking away.

Faith called after Odin, "Find Gabriel and tell him what has happened."

"When is he coming back?" asked Odin.

Lady Faith shrugged. Odin rolled his eyes for the second time. He wasn't a fan of any of the men in Lady Faith's life except for her offspring and, of course, their father.

# CHAPTER 38
# TOO LONG

*Back on Earth, in Waldmeer:*
It was a cool, still autumn evening as Faith-Amira and Rybert ascended the steep hill from Cypress Lane to Malik's house in Waldmeer. It was the house that Maria had been raised in, Amira had lived in once her parents died, and Faith had returned to from Borderfirma with her children. It was the Earth-home for three different identities of one oversoul.

"Malik owes me big time for bringing his mother back," joked Rybert.

As Faith and Rybert drew closer to the house, a silence fell over the two of them. And, it seemed, over all of Waldmeer.

Malik answered the doorbell, looked at the woman standing before him, dropped his tea, and put his arms out to her.

He said, almost inaudibly, "Twenty years, Mum."

Then, he cried.

# CROSSING LINES AND
# DRAWING CIRCLES

# CHAPTER 39
# BIRTHDAY BREAKDOWNS

## SOME BACKSTORY

I n *Borderfirma:*

When Gabriel travelled from Waldmeer to the inter-dimensional Borderfirma Lowlands twenty years ago, he was ready to give his relationship with Faith-Amira his best. For the first few years, he was somewhat dependent on her because he didn't know how to live in the inter-dimensional world on his own.

Gradually, he became accustomed to it. He made friends and found opportunities to follow his own leanings— including the ones that weren't particularly aligned with Faith's. After all, he was a different person to her. He always had been.

Faith and Gabriel stayed at Floating Cave Monastery for seven years until Aristotle and Indra turned twenty, married, and, as predicted by Nina's crystal ball, took over the management of the Lowlands.

Gabriel and Faith then went to live at the palace in the

Borderfirma Mountains. They did not live in the palace itself, although they were asked many times. They lived in one of the cottages on the grounds. Faith wouldn't let the palace staff into their home as she preferred to cook and clean herself. So, they let her be. And Gabriel and Faith also tried to let each other be. They had learned from experience that to do otherwise ended badly.

GABRIEL'S 40TH BIRTHDAY, *twenty years ago, on Earth, in Darnall:*

At the time of Gabriel's 40th birthday, he had moved from Amira's house in Waldmeer to Darnall. The *Boys of Darnall* decided to throw him a party at the local nightclub. Although it didn't seem a particularly good idea, Gabriel messaged Amira to invite her as he felt he couldn't not invite her to his fortieth.

As one would expect, it was a disaster. Amira thought that the drinking, noise, packed bodies, meaningless conversations, and blatant craving for human connection were the antithesis of who she was (and who anyone really was). *Nothing could be lonelier than that club,* she thought on the dark but reassuring road back to Waldmeer.

She told herself that if she and Gabriel were to be in each other's lives, it would have to be in neutral territory. She would not ask him to be more than he could or wanted to be. But nor would she be less than she was.

GABRIEL'S 50TH BIRTHDAY, *ten years ago, in the Borderfirma Lowlands:*

A decade later, in the Borderfirma Mountains, Gabriel's fiftieth was worse. Worse because it mattered more. In the months before his birthday, his behaviour towards Faith had deteriorated badly. Faith knew he was struggling, but she didn't know that he was planning a big party with his friends in the Lowlands, which she was neither invited to nor would she be informed of.

"Friends" is used loosely. It would be more accurate to say *drinking buddies*. Drinking buddies are not friends. They are either entertainment while one drinks or complicit drinkers who affirm the person's choice to do likewise.

The whole thing had crossed the line for Faith and caused a serious breakdown of their relationship.

A few months after the disastrous fiftieth party, Gabriel was near Floating Cave and decided to swim in the silent, salty pond. He always enjoyed being there. It was so relaxing. The old monk who lived in the Monastery was nowhere to be seen. As Gabriel floated, he heard the monk enter the cave.

After some friendly chit-chat, the monk said, "I hear you have hit a milestone birthday."

"Yeah," said Gabriel flatly.

He felt depressed. The inner dialogue, on repeat-play, started up again. *I didn't invite Amira because she hates drinking. And I didn't tell her because I have the right to do what I want.* No matter how many times it replayed, its compulsion to do so didn't lessen.

The monk drew two circles in the wet earth with a long stick. Next, he took a few steps further into the cave and drew two half-circles next to each other. He then drew two interlocking circles.

"Which do you prefer?" asked the monk.

As Gabriel wasn't sure what they were, he didn't answer.

"I don't like any of them," said the monk.

He pointed to the two single circles and said, "We are not meant to be alone."

He then pointed to the two half-circles and asked, "Do you want to give half of yourself to another person in order to make a whole unit?"

"God, no," said Gabriel.

The monk pointed to the two interlocking circles and said, "People try to make this work. They keep what they can of their own identity and merge as much of themselves with the other as they think is feasible or necessary."

"It's tolerable, I guess," said the monk. "But is tolerable good enough?"

Gabriel thought that it didn't feel like enough for him.

The monk drew two more single circles and a larger one enclosing both.

"This is happier," he said. "Neither person has to give any of themselves away. They are entirely themselves."

"I get it," said Gabriel. "Both circles are themselves."

Suddenly feeling much lighter, he added, "In the way that circles are themselves. And together, they live in something bigger than themselves—the circle enclosing both."

He was proud of himself for sounding so mature and brilliant.

"Correct," said the monk. "The large circle is something the two smaller circles belong to. Something they both merge with without losing anything. That is much less work and more pleasant, don't you think?"

When Gabriel left Floating Cave, he noticed that he no longer felt depressed. Instead, he felt quite hopeful and restored.

*That salt water does wonders,* he thought.

Instead of returning on the road back into the Lowlands, he took the opposite road to the Borderfirma Mountains. He was ready to try again.

BACK TO NOW IN *the Borderfirma Mountains:*

After so many breakdowns, Faith and Gabriel had no choice but to let each other be. They both came and went from their cottage on the grounds of the Borderfirma palace. They went to different places but returned to the same place, their shared home. And when they were both home, they were together.

# OUT OF THE PIT

# CHAPTER 40
# BARCODES OF LIFE

*n Store Creek:*

The winding country road between Store Creek and the highway was the best part of the two-hour drive to the city. Merlyn watched the morning light skip along the trees. The thin branch shadows on the road looked like a long line of barcodes.

*The mysterious barcodes of life,* thought Merlyn.

She felt content because, after all, who could not be at peace on such a beautiful morning? She remembered an Edgar Cayce saying that Enid often quoted,

*Happiness is your choice to make. How happy or how miserable do you want to be?*

She was on her way to Enid's house for one of her regular catch-ups with Edgar, which, in his ever-efficient way, he combined with checking on his mother's house. They met at the house and then walked around the corner to Pittstop.

Although Enid had been in the nursing home for over a year, Edgar had only recently put her house on the market. Merlyn did wonder, once the house was sold, if she and Edgar would find a new place to connect or if their friendship would fall into the pit of memories along with the house.

She recalled another of Enid's beloved Edgar Cayce quotes,

*We are attracted to another person at a soul level because by being with that individual, we are somehow provided with an impetus to become whole ourselves.*

As Merlyn pulled up at the house, she smiled at the hundreds of pansy seedlings planted at the beginning of winter. The house would be sold before the pansies had a chance to show their value. The new owner would probably pull them all out anyway because who has time for gardening these days?

Nevertheless, Edgar planted them as Enid had done for decades. Edgar was not a sentimental sort of person. Intelligent people don't tend to be sentimental. But there stood the neat rows of little flowers patiently waiting for winter to pass.

## CHAPTER 41
## NATURAL ORDER

*In Pittown:*

The owner of Pittstop fumbled some plates and somehow managed to catch them again.

"Good catch," said Merlyn.

"Yes, I'm a good catch," smiled the owner.

After their catch-up, Merlyn and Edgar parted company, and Merlyn headed for Edgar's Lake, at the bottom of the hill. She had to cross a busy intersection. Drivers in Pittown weren't normally polite. When Merlyn lived there, she heard them all day long honking their horns at the smallest indiscretions. However, when she navigated the crossing to the lake, she often met with gentlemanly behaviour.

A truck driver from the quarry stopped for her and nodded as if to say, *Why, of course. How else would one behave?*

Spotting the parent swans, Merlyn recalled the six cygnets she knew so well during her year in Pittown. She barely saw this past year's babies, and now they had grown and gone their separate ways.

*Strange,* thought Merlyn as she looked at the parent

swans, *how something can be fiercely protected with one's whole being. Then, life changes, and the valued thing is no longer a vital and intrinsic part of one's consciousness. For swans, it is the natural order.*

Deciding to walk the long way around the lake, Merlyn saw, in the distance, that Tom's unit was for sale. She hurried over as he was getting in his car.

"It's time to get out of the pit," said Tom. "Rybert is semi-retiring. He said he wants more time to go places and do stuff, so I'm going to Wurt Wurt Koort."

"What places?" asked Merlyn. "What stuff?"

"I'm not sure," said Tom. "He mumbled something about the mountains."

"Which mountains?" asked Merlyn.

"He said the ones near the border," said Tom. "Don't ask me. He didn't make sense."

"If you are in Wurt Wurt Koort, you will be near me in Store Creek," said Merlyn, clapping her hands.

It was mid-afternoon. Merlyn felt she should start driving back to Store Creek so she wouldn't be on the country stretch in the dark. What was delightful in the morning was less so at night.

As she got to her car, she took one final look at the pansies Edgar had planted. They seemed so vulnerable, all spaced out, with no connection to each other and nothing to protect them.

*You would think that it would be better to plant them in spring,* she thought. *Then they wouldn't have to suffer through winter. But maybe that's how they get strong.*

The winter solstice was a few days ago. As Merlyn pulled up at Nanna's House in Store Creek, the last light was disappearing over the farthest hill. Jumping out of the car to open the gate, she quickly got back in to avoid the blast of cold air.

She wondered how long it would take to get the fire going. Maybe she would just turn on the electric blanket and sit in bed.

It had been a long day.

## CHAPTER 42
## THE MARIAS

*In Waldmeer:*

Maria overheard her father and grandmother talking quietly one evening in the lounge room.

"I'm surprised that Gabriel hasn't already returned to Waldmeer, now that the portal is open again," said Malik.

"Me too," said Faith-Amira.

"He was dreaming of it many times," she added with one raised eyebrow.

After a while, she said, "I'd better go back and see how he's going."

Maria burst into the room and sat on her grandmother's lap. Although at thirteen, she was really too old for such things, she was such a slight girl that she easily fit on anyone's lap. Her young appearance and gentle, unassuming nature lulled one into the impression of her being much younger than her actual age.

"I'll go too," exclaimed Maria.

"Absolutely not," said Malik. "Off to bed."

Faith looked at him. There was a streak of panic in his

eyes. Maria sprang up and ran to her father. She tried to convince him that she would be safe and had always dreamed of going to a different place in the mountains. She often spoke to her parents about the faraway land that appeared in her dreams. Every time she mentioned it, another thread grew in Malik's protectiveness of her. Perhaps, also, another thread grew in his subconscious acknowledgement of the inevitable.

"Don't worry, Malik," said Faith, trying to pacify her son. "She can't come. We don't know if the portal will remain open. Anyone who goes may not be able to return for some time."

The next morning, Maria came from her room a different person.

"Dad, I have made my decision," she announced as if she had been asked to make one. "I'm going with Nannie."

Malik went into the back garden to remove himself from the conversation and his fears. He sat in their small orchard. It had been planted by his Earth grandfather, Lenny. Lenny also had a Maria who took her own path in life. That little Maria eventually turned into Malik's mother, Faith-Amira. He felt humbled that after his spiritually privileged upbringing and training, he was in the same position as his grandfather, who had none of that and met the same challenge in the same house, no less, with instinctive wisdom and love.

*It would have been harder for Grandfather Lenny,* thought Malik, *because he only knew Earth, but Earth is not my native home. I suppose if Grandfather Lenny could trust that his Maria would be okay, then I can, too.*

# SUMMARY OF
# WALDMEER SERIES

*A multi-generational journey of spiritual awakening, healing, and the spaces between worlds.*

Beneath the surface of an idyllic coastal village, unseen forces stir. Waldmeer is a place where the visible and invisible meet—where inter-dimensional realms brush against everyday life, and where emotional truths rise quietly but undeniably.

Told across seven books, the *Waldmeer Series* follows Maria–Amira from the groundedness of her rural home to the doorways into higher realms of perception and spiritual transformation. Around her, those she loves and seeks to help are drawn into their own awakenings, resistances, and reckonings.

Waldmeer moves between ordinary moments and otherworldly initiations. Between earthly love and higher love. Between who we think we are... and what we truly are.

At times tender, at times confronting, these stories unfold in layers—personal, relational, and metaphysical.

# ABOUT THE AUTHOR

*On the beach at Lorne, Australia (the coastal village Waldmeer is based on).*

**Donna Goddard** is a spiritual author whose work blends clarity, devotion, and metaphysical insight. With 25+ published books across spiritual nonfiction, fiction, poetry, and children's literature, she writes to uplift consciousness and offer healing through words.

Donna's Facebook author page has over 400,000 followers worldwide, and her YouTube channel has received 4 million views. Her books are read by spiritual seekers globally and are known for their honesty, poetic style, and transformative energy.

Her writing is an offering—to help others awaken their own inner spirit, trust its guidance, and create a life of depth, beauty, and quiet joy.

All links at https://linktr.ee/donnagoddard

## Ratings and Reviews

Donna would be grateful for any ratings or reviews.

# ALSO BY DONNA GODDARD

**Fiction**
*Waldmeer Series: A Spiritual Fiction Series*
*Nanima Series: Spiritual Fiction*
*Enanika Series: Visionary Fiction*
*Riverland Series (children's fiction 6 to 9 years)*
*Foxie (children's fiction 7 to 12 years)*

**Nonfiction**
*Love and Devotion Series*
*Sweet Spirit Series*
*Consciousness Series*
*Being Meditation Series*
*Many Moments Series*
*Poetry Series*
*Love's Longing*
*Dance: A Spiritual Affair*
*Writing: A Spiritual Voice*

www.ingramcontent.com/pod-product-compliance
Lightning Source LLC
Chambersburg PA
CBHW020524120726
47904CB00003B/960